7 NISSAN

Scale 1:40000

Projection: Geographic
Datum: WGS 84
Ellipsoid: WGS 84
Date: April 2003

SUITABLE FOR REFERENCE PURPOSES ONLY

Names and boundary representation
are not necessarily authoritative.

Proper names on this product may not conform
to standard NIMA product specifications and
U.S. Board on Geographic Names standards.

(c) COPYRIGHT 2003 BY THE
UNITED STATES GOVERNMENT

NO COPYRIGHT CLAIMED UNDER TITLE 17 U.S.C.

ISBN-13: 978-0615956954 (shutupyeats.net)

ISBN-10: 0615956955

For:

SFC Ricardo D. Young
1978-2013

SSG Solomon Sam
1982-2008

and all of the others.

"Although the U.S. military contiunues to assess the situation in Mosul ahead of a June 30th deadline to withdraw troops from population centers, President Barack Obama said that the recent increase in violence won't affect his plan for a phased military withdrawal. Friday's attack was the deadliest . . . "

Meanwhile . . .

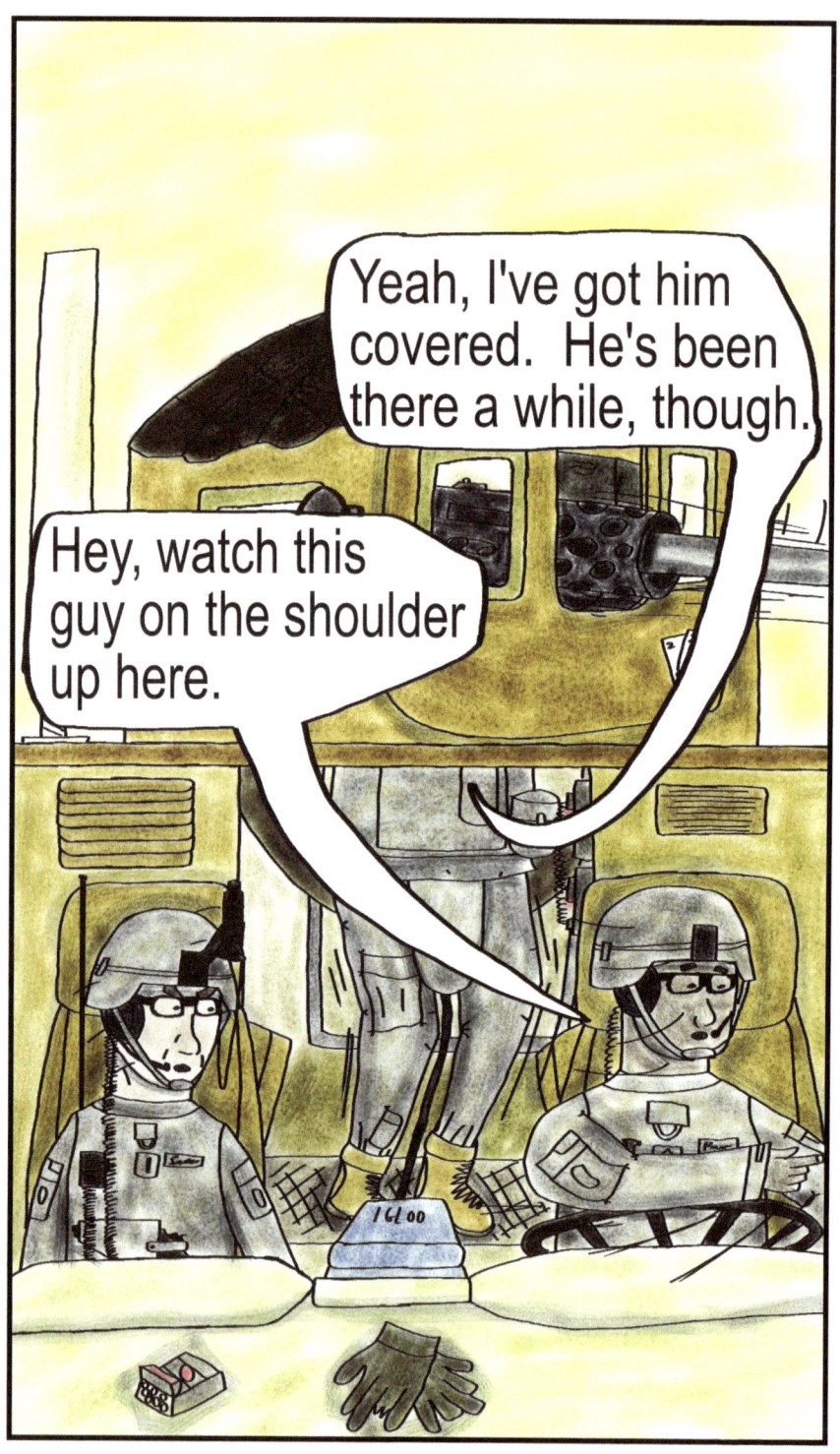

Send and . . . send.
There. Done!

Platoon Perstat   NMC Vehicles

Status	Name	Status	BN	ISSUE
P	SSG(P)h-	P	207	Transmission
USACE	SGT h	OLV	204	Is AN RG33Lt
OLV	SPC mj	P	222	on fire
P	SPC V-	P	218	Hydraulic leak CLΞΞ
WIA/EVAC	SPC Us	P		
P	PFC m	P		
P	PV2 G-	EXTRA DUTY		
P	PVT h-	EXTRA DUTY		
P				

SECRET

175 m

SEND

Fig. 3: Pen Flare Fired

At approximately 141649AUG08 Badger Red 4 fired a pen flare at the oncoming vehicle at range of approximately 175 meters. It struck the pavement approximately five meters in front the vehicle, which was moving at approximately 35 mph. The vehicle then turned 180 degr and returned the way it came. Badger Red then continued mission.

UNCLASSIFIED

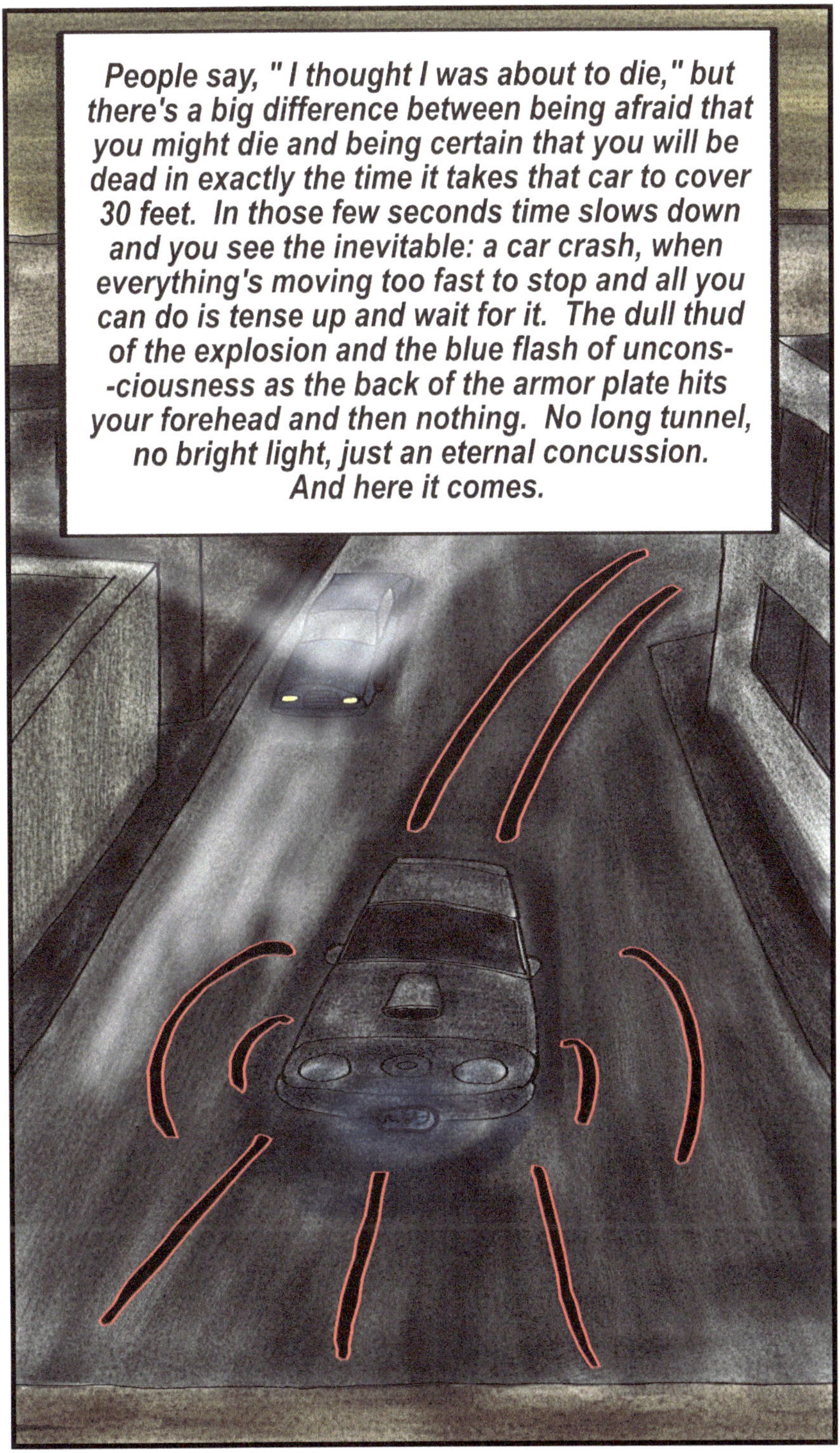

People say, "I thought I was about to die," but there's a big difference between being afraid that you might die and being certain that you will be dead in exactly the time it takes that car to cover 30 feet. In those few seconds time slows down and you see the inevitable: a car crash, when everything's moving too fast to stop and all you can do is tense up and wait for it. The dull thud of the explosion and the blue flash of uncons--ciousness as the back of the armor plate hits your forehead and then nothing. No long tunnel, no bright light, just an eternal concussion. And here it comes.

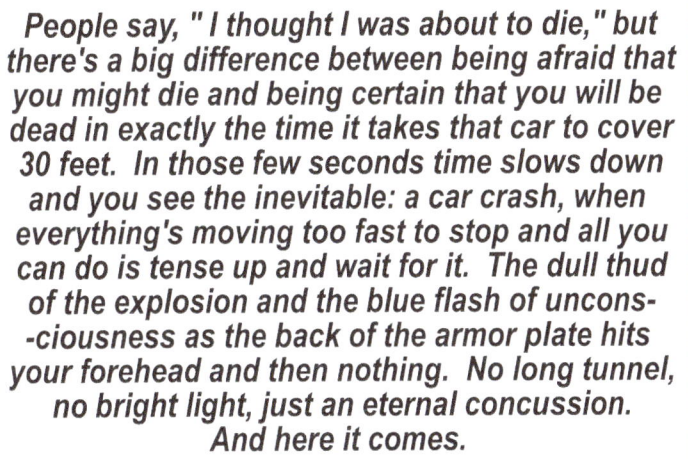

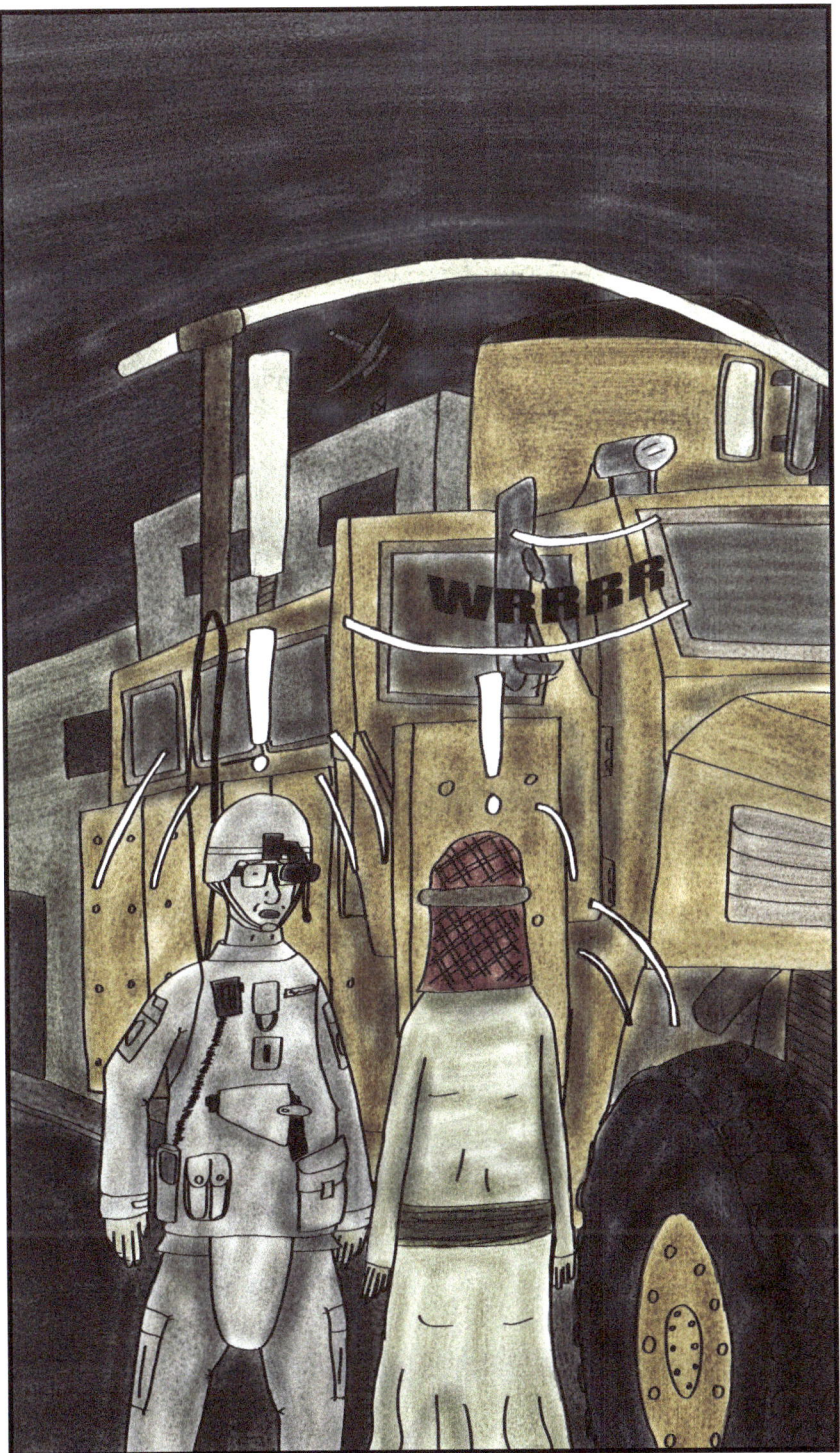

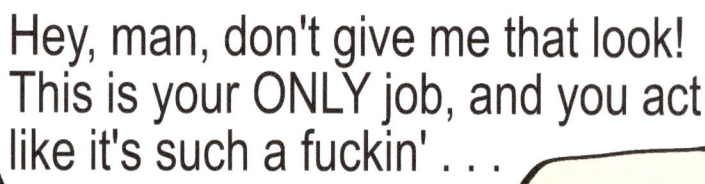

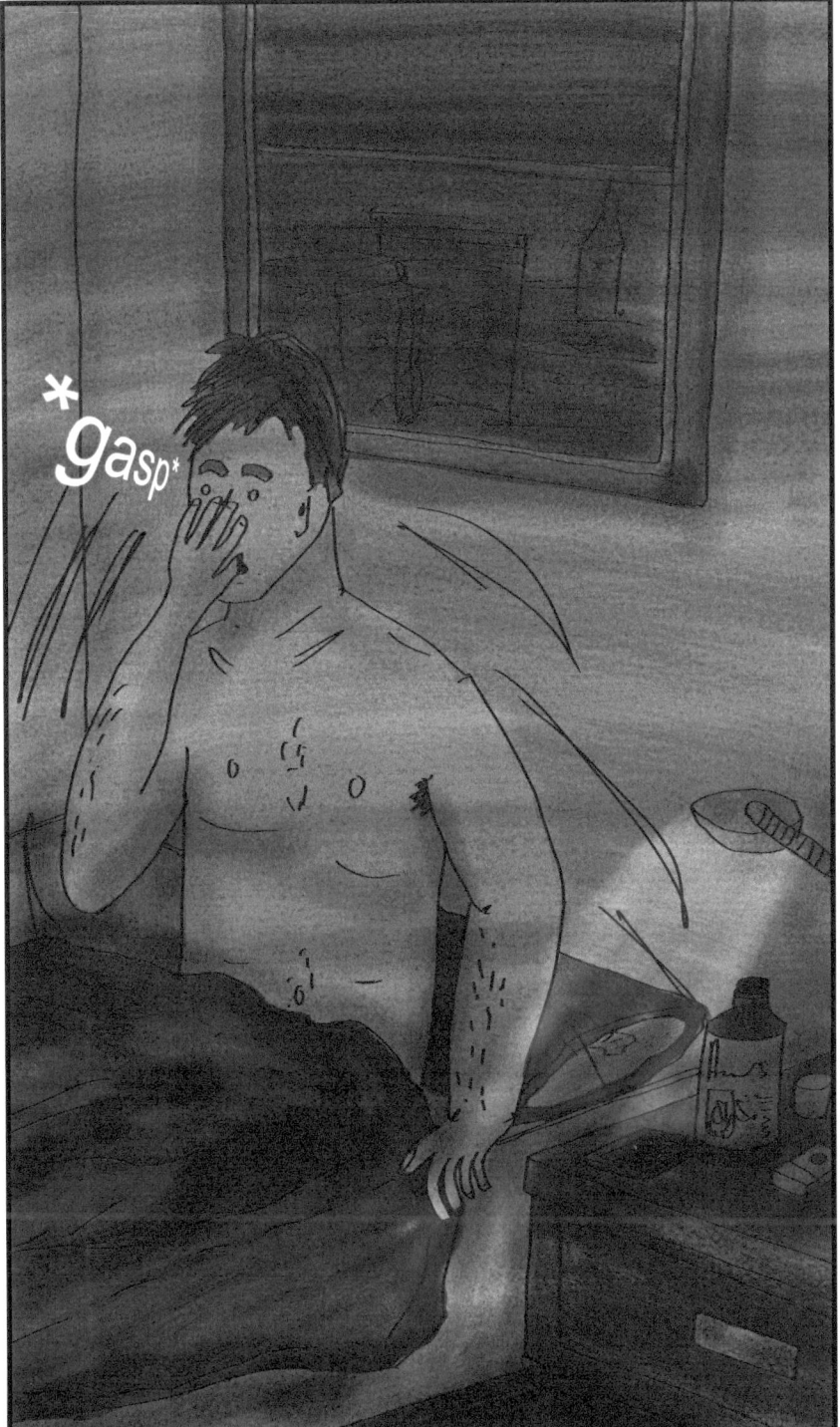

The end.

Glossary

The U.S. Army uses a sometimes bewildering array of official and unofficial acronyms and slang, which are nevertheless ignored only at the cost of authenticity.

7. Radio call signs: used in this story are generic peacetime ones. Deployed military units create their own. "6" as a suffix implies that the user is the officer in charge; "7" implies a noncommissioned officer in charge. Other numbers indicate a subordinate unit, or staff section.

8. TOC: Tactical Operations Center. The unit's permanently manned headquarters, where the commander may or may not be located.

8. BFT: Blue Force Tracker. Electronic hardware and software that displays the location of U.S. vehicles on a moving map display.

8. SP / RP: n. Start Point / Rally Point. v. To depart from the start point on a mission and to arrive at a designated halt, or rally point, during or at the end of a mission.

15. Roads and neighborhoods: principal roads and neighborhoods were assigned English names to reduce confusion, especially where the Arabic name was dificult to pronounce or unclear. In Mosul, these were typically automobile brands, for no particular reason. MSR and ASR stand for Main and Auxiliary Suply Route. MSR Tampa became well known, being the main highway running the length of Iraq from Basra to Mosul.

16. CONOP: Concept of Operations. The plan for the mission, to be reviewed by the Commander before it begins.

20. DFAC: Dining facility.

25. Like all contractors in Iraq since the dawn of time, this guy is Turkish.

29. Interpreters get code names for their own protection.

54. VBIED: Vehicle Borne Improvised Explosive Device; a car or truck bomb.

90. AR 670-1: Wear and Appearance of Army Uniforms and Insignia -- also covers subjects like nail polish.

91. AAR: After Action Review -- a "lessons learned" discussion after an operation.

92: Tropic Lightning Hero: 25th Infantry Division initiative to recognize individual, low-ranking Soldiers who did something extrordinary. Each platoon submitts one PowerPoint slide a week with a picture of a Soldier and description of his/her accomplishments. These are filtered up to a staff officer who picks the winner, whose slide is printed, stapled to a wall somewhere and forgotten about. The flaw in the system is that the number of slides generated dramatically exceeds the number of Soldiers who have in fact done anything out of the ordinary.

Soldiers' efforts see success in former insurgent stronghold

March 14, 2009

Pfc. Sharla Perrin, 3rd HBCT, 1st Cav. Div. Public Affairs MND-N

MOSUL, Iraq - Mosul has often been referred to as the last haven of insurgent activity in Iraq, but lately the city has had fewer doors bashed in and more tender loving care.

Col. Greg Maxton, the deputy commanding officer of the 3rd Heavy Brigade Combat Team, 1st Cavalry Division, has been sitting "shotgun" with the residential, military and government leaders of Mosul since mid-February coordinating projects to clean the city's streets of trash. Although Maxton oversees all non-lethal operations in Ninewah province, there are other bricks in the pathway to success in the area.

Executed at the lowest possible level, companies, batteries and troops within 3rd HBCT have worked with local Iraqi leaders to establish the clean-up projects to turn what were once neighborhoods laden with the weight of their filth into communities thriving with physical and emotional potential.

After agreements are made and meetings are adjourned, the junior officers that command these lowest-level units watch the ideals go into action in the Mosul neighborhoods.

"The work that they're doing is spectacular," Maxton said. "We just have to keep our minds open; anything is possible." When contemplating projects Maxton poses the question - - "What does it take to promote a better environment for the people who live there'"

"Some of the companies may not realize the foundation of what they're doing, but really, everything hinges on it, and they're doing a great job," said Maxton.

7 Nissan is a neighborhood in northern Mosul that is supervised by Battery B., 2nd Bn., 82nd Field Artillery Regiment, 3rd HBCT.

A month ago, the neighborhood's empty lots and curbside gutters were riddled with an assortment of garbage from plastic grocery bags to broken-down cars. On March 7, Capt. Derrick Burden, the battery's commander, circulated the area and saw clean sidewalks, freshly swept streets and local residents spending their Saturday afternoon picking up trash and spreading gravel.

"My greatest achievement in this mission is watching [hired residents] come to work at seven in the morning every day," Burden said. "The people of 7 Nissan talk about how the government is doing a good job of hiring people within the neighborhood to work."

The work Burden and his battery have done is the solution to more than just aesthetic value and employment. In the past, unemployed men in Mosul were becoming puppets for the insurgent force as a means to provide for their families. As these same men have been provided a legitimate source of income, the illicit organizations for which they used to work will no longer be a source of strength. The efforts of 3rd HBCT will ultimately drive insurgents away.

If Iraq were a dense forest, these projects are rays of light reaching to infant saplings struggling to grow amidst the undergrowth. Holding a job and providing for their families gives the men of 7 Nissan special pride in themselves and a start at a return to normalcy. The city has been oppressed by the war and its effects for upwards of six years, and for some, that has meant six years since the shop that was their main source of income was destroyed in a suicide bomber incident.

What used to be a job designated for the lowest rung on the social ladder is now widely accepted, as most of Mosul has been reduced to abject poverty since the start of the war.

"Having a job and a legitimate way to earn an income is very important," Maxton was told by one worker. "Honestly, I'm doing it in my own neighborhood. These are my brothers that are next to me picking up trash."

"I think that's the great part about keeping it within the neighborhoods," Maxton said. "They are taking ownership and pride in the work they are accomplishing."

Keith Schnell joined the U.S. Army in 2007 and served in Iraq from 2008-2009. This is his first graphic novel.

www.shutupyeats.net